An elderly emperor had a plan.

He ordered all of the children to his garden.

They were given a pot and a seed.

"Come back in the summer," he said. "Bring me the best tree and you will be emperor."

Ling took his pot and seed. He went back to his house.

Ling added soil to the pot.

He popped the seed in.

Ling kept the pot in the garden.

The seed had plenty of sun and rain.

Ling waited and waited. But the seed did not sprout.

In the summer, Ling and the rest of the children went back to the emperor.

All of the children apart from Ling had trees.

“I feel silly,” Ling said, standing next to his empty pot.

Suddenly, the emperor pointed at Ling.

“You are the winner,” he said.

“A good emperor never lies. I had boiled the seeds to stop them sprouting.”

Ling lived happily as an emperor. He was indeed good and just.